MW01143417

WRITERS REPUBLIC

Copyright © 2020 by Christiane Dutrisac.

All rights reserved. No part of this book may be reproduced in any form or by any electronic or mechanical means, including information storage and retrieval systems, without permission in writing from the publisher, except by reviewers, who may quote brief passages in a review.

This publication contains the opinions and ideas of its author. It is intended to provide helpful and informative material on the subjects addressed in the publication. The author and publisher specifically disclaim all responsibility for any liability, loss, or risk, personal or otherwise, which is incurred as a consequence, directly or indirectly, of the use and application of any of the contents of this book.

WRITERS REPUBLIC L.L.C.
515 Summit Ave. Unit R1
Union City, NJ 07087, USA

Website: *www.writersrepublic.com*
Hotline: *1-877-656-6838*
Email: *info@writersrepublic.com*

Ordering Information:
Quantity sales. Special discounts are available on quantity purchases by corporations, associations, and others. For details, contact the publisher at the address above.

Library of Congress Control Number:		2020924648
ISBN-13:	978-1-64620-809-8	[Paperback Edition]
	978-1-64620-810-4	[Digital Edition]

Rev. date: 12/01/2020

This book was written to thank all those who have helped me along the way. I appreciate you all! To all those living with a medical condition, don't be afraid to ask for and accept others' help. To all those living with Wolfram Syndrome, don't lose hope. Good things are coming our way!

« Star light, star bright
First star I see tonight
I wish I may, I wish I might
Have this wish I wish tonight.
I wish for one boy who will love me forever. »

As Josie climbed down from her windowsill, she
tumbled to the ground and to her unpleasant
surprise, her eyes popped out of their sockets. She
cried out in fear: « Help, help! I lost my eyes! »

Just then, her friend Ally came rushing in. « Josie, I found them! » To Josie's relief, Ally helped put them back in. « Thank you so much! » said Josie. « I feel so much better thanks to you! »

Later that day, Josie was playing outside with some friends when her nose began to itch.

« Ah, ah, ah, atchoo! » Josie sneezed, fell to her knees and saw her nose bounce away from her.

Before she had time to react, her friend Stanley caught it. Josie ran to him. « Thank you my hero! You saved my nose! » « I thought I was catching the ball! » he chuckled.

That evening, she invited her friends for dinner. When her dish was ready, she immediately took a bite. Before she could taste what she was about to serve, her taste buds flew away to avoid the heat.

« I'll try it for you! » said Ally as she blew to cool it down. « Mmm..delicious! » « Thank you so much Ally! I don't know what I would've done without you! » replied Josie relieved of the taste-test.

The three friends found themselves at the park again, in a final attempt to play before nightfall. As the girls were swinging, Stanley was sliding. Without anyone noticing, a bat flew into Ally's hair.

« Aaah! » yelled Ally very loudly. Josie's ears reacted quickly to the sound. They immediately curled up and closed so as not to let the sound enter. Stanley came to their rescue scaring the bat away.

As they began walking home, Josie noticed her friends waving their arms and moving their lips but she couldn't hear them. Her ears were still blocked. Pointing to her ears, she started to cry.

Her friends both came to her sides, massaging her ears to open them. Feeling at ease, she thanked them again. « No need to thank us Josie. We'll always be here for you! » replied Stanley.

Ally added: « Don't forget Josie, when all your other senses fail you, your touch will always save the day! » Just then, Stanley pulled Josie in to give her a hug. « I wished upon a star! » thought Josie.

Thank you for purchasing and reading this book.

All proceeds from the sale of this book will help fund the research and trials being conducted by Dr. Fumihiko Urano and his team at Washington University in St. Louis, Missouri. Know that we truly appreciate all of your hard work and efforts. Thanks to you all, we are hopeful and look forward for things to come!

For more information, visit: wolframsyndrome.dom.wustl.edu

Christiane Dutrisac is a Wolfram Syndrome survivor who wants to bring hope to children bearing the burden of this condition. Just as the main character Josie loses the use of each of her senses except touch, Christiane is losing her senses due to WS.

Her talented 10 year old daughter, Sophie, is aspiring to be an artist one day and makes a beautiful contribution to this project. Many thanks to you Sophie!

CPSIA information can be obtained
at www.ICGtesting.com
Printed in the USA
LVHW020608050221
678409LV00001B/1

Copyright © 2020 by Christiane Dutrisac.

All rights reserved. No part of this book may be reproduced in any form or by any electronic or mechanical means, including information storage and retrieval systems, without permission in writing from the publisher, except by reviewers, who may quote brief passages in a review.

This publication contains the opinions and ideas of its author. It is intended to provide helpful and informative material on the subjects addressed in the publication. The author and publisher specifically disclaim all responsibility for any liability, loss, or risk, personal or otherwise, which is incurred as a consequence, directly or indirectly, of the use and application of any of the contents of this book.

WRITERS REPUBLIC L.L.C.
515 Summit Ave. Unit R1
Union City, NJ 07087, USA

Website: *www.writersrepublic.com*
Hotline: *1-877-656-6838*
Email: *info@writersrepublic.com*

Ordering Information:
Quantity sales. Special discounts are available on quantity purchases by corporations, associations, and others. For details, contact the publisher at the address above.

Library of Congress Control Number: 2020924648
ISBN-13:   978-1-64620-809-8   [Paperback Edition]
                  978-1-64620-810-4   [Digital Edition]

Rev. date: 12/01/2020

Ce livre a été écrit pour remercier tous ceux qui m'ont aidé tout au long de ce trajet. Je vous apprécie tous! À tous ceux qui vivent avec une condition médicale, n'ayez pas peur de demander ou d'accepter l'aide des autres. À tous ceux vivant avec le syndrome de Wolfram, ne perdez pas espoir. L'avenir nous réserve de belles surprises!

« Étoile brillante, étoile filante
Première étoile que je rencontre
Je souhaite avoir, je souhaite pouvoir
Obtenir ce souhait ce soir.
Je souhaite qu'un garçon m'aimera pour toujours. »

Alors que Josie descendait de sa fenêtre, elle tomba sur le sol et, à sa surprise désagréable, ses yeux sortirent de leurs orbites. Elle cria de peur: « Au secours, au secours! Je ne trouve pas mes yeux! »

Ce fut à ce moment que son amie Ally entra
précipitamment. « Josie, je les ai trouvés! » Au
grand soulagement de Josie, Ally aida à les
remettre en place. « Merci beaucoup! » dit Josie.
« Je me sens tellement mieux grâce à toi! »

Plus tard dans la journée, Josie jouait à l'extérieur avec des amis lorsque son nez commença à piquer. « Ah, ah, ah, atchoum! » Josie éternua, tomba à genoux et vit son nez rebondir loin d'elle.

Avant d'avoir le temps de réagir, son ami Stanley le saisit. Josie courut vers lui. « Merci mon héros! Tu as sauvé mon nez! » « Je pensais attraper le ballon! » dit-il en riant.

Ce soir-là, elle invita ses amis à souper. Quand son plat fut prêt, elle prit aussitôt une bouchée. Avant qu'elle puisse goûter ce qu'elle allait servir, ses papilles se sont envolées pour éviter la chaleur.

« Je vais l'essayer pour toi! » dit Ally alors qu'elle soufflait pour le refroidir. Elle ajouta sans hésiter: « Miam, délicieux! » « Merci beaucoup Ally! Je ne sais pas ce que je ferais sans toi! » répondit Josie, soulagée du test de goût.

Les trois amis se retrouvèrent de nouveau au parc, dans une dernière tentative de jouer avant la tombée de la nuit. Alors que les filles se balançaient, Stanley glissait. Personne ne remarqua lorsqu'une chauve-souris vola dans les cheveux d'Ally.

« Aaah! » cria-t-elle fortement. Les oreilles de Josie réagirent rapidement au son. Elles s'enroulèrent et fermèrent aussitôt pour ne pas laisser le son entrer. Stanley vint à leur secours en chassant la chauve-souris.

Alors qu'ils se dirigeaient vers la maison, Josie remarqua que ses amis agitaient les bras et remuaient les lèvres, mais elle ne pouvait pas les entendre. Ses oreilles étaient toujours bloquées. Elle pointa à ses oreilles et se mit à pleurer.

Ses deux amis s'approchèrent d'elle et massèrent ses oreilles pour les ouvrir. Elle se sentit soulagée et les remercia encore. « Pas besoin de nous remercier Josie. Nous serons toujours là pour toi! » répondit Stanley.

Ally ajouta: « N'oublie pas Josie, quand tous tes autres sens te feront défaut, ton toucher sauvera toujours le jour! ». À ce moment-là, Stanley tira Josie vers lui et la prit dans ses bras.

« J'ai souhaité sur une étoile! » pensa Josie.

Merci d'avoir acheté et d'avoir lu ce livre.

Tous les profits de la vente de ce livre aideront à financer la recherche et les essais mené par Dr. Fumihiko Urano et son équipe à l'Université de Washington à St. Louis, Missouri. Sachez que nous apprécions véritablement tout votre travail ardue et vos efforts. Grâce à vous tous, nous gardons espoir et nous avons hâte à ce qui viendra! Pour plus d'information, visitez: wolframsyndrome.dom.wustl.edu

Christiane Dutrisac est une survivante du syndrome de Wolfram qui veut donner de l'espoir aux enfants portant le fardeau de cette condition. Tout comme le personnage principal Josie perd l'utilisation de chacun de ses sens sauf le toucher, Christiane perd ses sens à cause du syndrome de Wolfram.

Sa fille talentueuse, Sophie, est âgée de 10 ans. Elle espère être artiste un jour et fait une belle contribution à ce projet. Merci maintes fois Sophie!